COSIMO CAT

Kenneth Oppel
Regolo Ricci

North Winds Press
A division of Scholastic Canada Ltd.

To Philippa — contra mundum.
K.O.

To Mario.
R.R.

Canadian Cataloguing in Publication Data

Oppel, Kenneth
    Cosimo cat

ISBN 0-590-73649-3

I. Ricci, Regolo.   II. Title.

PS8579.P64C6B 1991   jC813'.54   C90-095178-8
PZ7.0614Co 1991

6 5 4 3 2 1   Printed in Hong Kong   0 1 2 3 4 5/9

owan looked up at the sign stapled to the telephone pole.

MISSING: CAT
CHARCOAL GREY, COBALT BLUE EYES
ANSWERS TO THE NAME OF COSIMO.
REWARD.

Rowan read the sign once more and then ran back down the street toward home.

Upstairs in his bedroom he rummaged through his closet and blew dust off his adventure gear.

"What's up?" his father asked, looking in.

"Missing cat," Rowan told him.

"Ah," said his father.

"What colour is cobalt blue?" Rowan wanted to know.

"Cobalt blue? Deep, deep blue, ocean blue, summer sky blue."

"Thanks," Rowan said, walking down the stairs toward the door.

"Will you be back in time for supper?" his father called after him.

Outside, Rowan switched on the cat detector he had made from old radio parts. Strong signals were coming from down the alley. He came to the abandoned coach house, with its sagging walls and tar paper windows and broad wooden doors with huge hinges. A slate shingle slid clattering off the roof and landed with a muffled thud in the mud.

The cat detector was beeping like mad. Rowan cautiously pushed open one of the doors. Inside, there was darkness and the smell of wood and oil and long-ago horses and hay. Rowan fumbled for his flashlight and switched it on.

There were cats everywhere, hundreds of them. They were stretched out on the floor like lazy lions, they were perched on shelves and tables, they were draped along the rafters. Their heads turned toward Rowan, and their eyes glittered like glass marbles in the beam of his flashlight.

The cat detector made a popping sound and sent up a curl of smoke. It had been completely overloaded. Rowan swallowed hard. He felt strange and awkward in the midst of all the cats.

There were cats of all shapes and colours, cats with spare-tire bellies, cats with their ribs showing. There were white cats and black cats, cats with stripes and splotches, but none that was charcoal grey with cobalt blue eyes.

"Have any of you seen Cosimo?" Rowan asked quietly.

The cats watched him in silence.

Before Rowan could back out of the coach house, there was a flash of blue that made him gasp. It was a flash of cobalt blue eyes in the darkness, a deep, deep blue, ocean blue, summer sky blue. Rowan glimpsed a charcoal grey cat just as it disappeared through a gap in the wall.

Outside the coach house, Rowan found tracks in the damp mud. He took out his magnifying glass. They were definitely cat paw prints. He followed them down the alley and past the corner store to the park.

Rowan could see a cat drinking from the fountain.

"Cosimo," he called, moving closer.

The cat looked over its shoulder at Rowan and then sprang away across the freshly mown grass.

W here's he off to? Rowan wondered as he ran to keep up. He dashed through the park gates and found himself on a busy downtown street.

The noise from the city swirled around Rowan's ears. He pulled binoculars out of his knapsack and scanned the street. There was no sign of Cosimo.

A group of people on the sidewalk had stopped and were pointing up into the air. Rowan looked up too.

ight stories above the street, Cosimo was walking along a narrow ledge on the outside of a building. Pigeons fluttered away in alarm. Higher up on the wall of the building was a huge billboard with a picture of a beautiful stone cat. It had emerald green eyes, deep, deep green, seaweed green, summer grass green. Underneath the picture of the cat was written:

COME AND SEE A 2500-YEAR-OLD CAT
AT THE MUSEUM

Cosimo gazed up at the billboard, took a good look, and then stepped nimbly through an open window.

owan burst into the building. Three businesswomen moved to one
side as he marched toward the elevator. He stepped inside and pushed
a button. As the doors were closing he saw Cosimo walking calmly
down the stairs, but it was too late. The elevator doors snapped shut
and he was lifted to the eighth floor. By the time he got back down,
Cosimo was gone.

"He went that way," one of the women said, pointing out into the
street.

"Thanks," said Rowan, running through the doors.

At the steps of the subway, he found a cat collar. Cosimo's name and address were written across it. Rowan looked around but didn't see the cat anywhere.

"He went that way," said a man playing a bassoon on the corner. "Down into the subway."

It was a free-for-all on the escalators, everyone pushing and shoving to get to the trains. On the platform, a man sang opera. Rowan couldn't see a thing through the crowd. The train arrived in a blast of noise and warm air. He was pushed inside by the crowd and the doors crashed shut.

As the train raced through the tunnel, the lights blinked out for a second and Rowan thought he saw a flash of blue at the far end of the car: deep, deep blue, ocean blue, summer sky blue.

"Hey!" someone yelled when the lights came back on. "There's a cat in here."

"How did it get onto the subway?" someone else said.

"Who knows, but here it is," another voice answered.

"Did it pay?" a concerned lady wanted to know.

"Just shoo it out at the next station," instructed a man with a big voice. "We can't have cats on our public transit system."

The train screeched to a standstill at the next station and Rowan got off just in time to see Cosimo disappear up the escalator through a forest of legs.

Rowan pushed through the swinging glass doors into the underground shopping mall. He zigzagged through the crowd. He passed brightly lit shop fronts. He smelled a thousand different food smells coming from the underground restaurants. He wrinkled his nose. It was too much.

"Excuse me," Rowan asked a shopkeeper, "but did you see a cat pass by?"

"A cat!" the man said.

"Charcoal grey," Rowan explained, "with cobalt blue eyes."

"What would a cat be doing in an underground shopping mall?" exclaimed the shopkeeper. "That's the craziest thing I ever heard! Of course I didn't see a cat pass by."

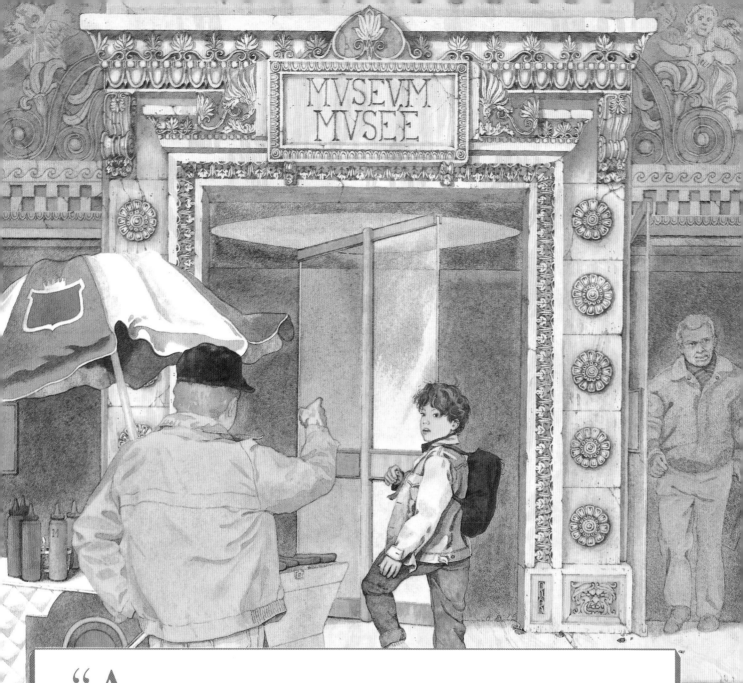

"A cat just passed by," said one of the shop clerks, looking out into the mall. "He went that way."

A glass elevator rocketed Rowan up out of the underground mall and back onto the street.

The museum was across the road. Rowan remembered the billboard.

"He went that way," a man selling hot dogs said, pointing.

"I know," Rowan told him. He climbed the stone steps and swirled through the revolving doors.

Inside it was very quiet. Whispers floated through the air. He was standing in the middle of an enormous hallway with high ceilings and marble floors.

Then he heard it.

He held his breath and listened hard.

There it was again, as faint as the whisper of the sea on a calm day.

It was a cat's purr.

Rowan started down a long hallway. The purring was getting louder. He walked into the Egyptian gallery filled with glass cases and statues.

15

I n the centre of the room, on a high pedestal, were two stone cats. They sat facing one another, still as stone. Rowan couldn't tell them apart. He stepped softly closer. The purring was coming from the statues.

One of the cats had emerald green eyes, deep, deep green, seaweed green, summer grass green. And the other cat had eyes of cobalt blue, deep, deep blue, ocean blue, summer sky blue.

"Cosimo," Rowan said quietly, and the cat with the cobalt eyes turned and looked at the boy. "Don't you want to go home?"

Cosimo looked back at the stone cat, nuzzled against it quickly, and then stepped off the pedestal into the boy's waiting arms. As he turned to leave, Rowan thought he saw the whiskers on the Egyptian cat quiver a little.

18

owan strode back the way he had come, through the underground
mall, onto the squealing subway, along the bustling streets of the city,
across the park with the fountain, up the alley past the coach house,
and toward a small brick house with a front porch.

"I found your cat," he told the woman who answered the door.

She smiled at Rowan as she look Cosimo from his arms. "She's done this before, you know," she told Rowan. "She just disappears for days at a time."

"It's a she?" Rowan said. "I thought it was a he."

"It's hard to tell with cats, isn't it?"

Cosimo pushed out of the woman's arms and sprang into the house. Rowan felt sad to see her go.

"I found her in the museum," he told the woman.

"How odd. She's just had kittens, you know, so maybe she needed a nice break. Do you have a kitten of your own?"

Rowan shook his head, hoping she would ask.

"Would you like one, as your reward?" she asked. "They're old enough to leave their mother now."

"I'd love one," Rowan told her.

He waited in the front hallway as she went into the next room. Rowan could hear kittens mewing through the walls. The woman returned with a tiny grey kitten in her cupped hands.

"Thank you for finding Cosimo," she said. "Was it much trouble?"

"Not really," Rowan said with a grin.

On the way down the street toward home, he looked into the kitten's eyes. One was cobalt blue, deep, deep blue, ocean blue, summer sky blue. And the other was emerald green, deep, deep green, seaweed green, summer grass green.